OPERATION MISSING BOY

FIRST MISSION OF THE FAB FOUR

VINOD BHASKAR

Made with ❤ on the Notion Press Platform
www.notionpress.com

Dedicate to,

Ibne Safi, Vedprkash Kamboj, Enid Blyton, Sir Arthur Conan Doyle, Earl Stanley Gardner, James Hadley Chase, Agatha Christie, and Alistair Maclean, Whose novels I used to read from childhood to till date.

Contents

Foreword

Foreword

It is a detective novel; whose heroes are youngsters. This is the first novel of a series. In this series, these heroes will encounter an assignment and solve it. To solve the case, they will undoubtedly face life risks. And as you know, life-threatening is a part of the detecting job. The other intention of these novels is to be interesting for teenagers or who are weaker in English, so that young readers may get used to reading and enjoy it and learn English in this way. Anyway, read and enjoy.

Acknowledgements

Copywriting: Vinod Bhaskar
Copyright: Vinod Bhaskar
Editor: Ronit Kanjan

Operation Missing Boy

First Mission of the Fab Four

by

Vinod Bhaskar

A novel of child detectives for younger readers

CHAPTER ONE

1

"The husband ate the dinner in the darkness of the night and in the morning he was no more." Hameed was telling a detective story to the Fab Four team, Vijay, Arhan, Balwant, and Miss Marple. "This story was told me, by Mr. Nevandram, my Mama (maternal uncle) when I was in our village."

"Uncle, Mr. Nevandram was your Mama?" Miss Marple asked.

"Oh, come on Marple, in those days all people in India, particularly in villages, are brothers, sisters, uncles, aunties. In that way, I called him Mama. He was an excellent person, always wearing a white half-shirt and pajamas. I'll tell you about him later. Or why later, one incidence I'll tell you now, detective story can wait for a few minutes.

"One day there was a fight between two vegetable vendors in the locality. One of them, Vinod Shukla, the young one, beat up the other vendor, Pohumal, who was a little older. Pohumal lodged a complaint with the police. Mama came to know this. He went to the police station. He met the PI, who was the station-in-charge and asked about the fighting complaint in his locality. Inspector called a constable and ordered him to bring the report. When he brought the report, the inspector gave it to Mama. Mama looked at it one minute and said to the inspector, '"They both are our brethren,"' and he tore up the report and threw it away.

"Inspector said, '"Arre..."' But the report was already torn up, so he further said nothing. And interestingly, you don't believe it. Pohumal belongs to Mama's society, yet he tore his report. Mama was so great.

"Now come to the story, recited to me by the great Mama. The husband was a laborer and worked in the city. He used to return late evening, get rest for a while, and then ate dinner. There was no electricity in those days, so people used to light lamps, but the husband and wife were very poor, so it was often dark in their hut. That day also he ate his dinner in the dark, and he met his death. He was young, robust; in today's language, a six-pack man, and used to enter the arena. So his death was the talk of the town. Everyone was shocked. The Police Patel of the village reported to the police station because everyone thought he must be poisoned.

"The following story should not be considered a short story in the traditional sense. It is simply the story of a strange and daring experiment that was once attempted. It is made available to people who are curious about the unknowable possibilities of the hereafter.

"When my Mama told me this story, we were at the Chaupal (Meeting place in villages). You may say it is the oldest form of clubs." Hameed further said, "Other people presented at the chaupal were also listening to the story. The police came from the town. The police inspector arrested the wife on the charges of murder. Obviously, she was crying, '"I did nothing,"' but her voice fell on deaf ears.

"In those days, post-mortem and the forensic lab were not even imagined in India. Inspector fetched her to the police station. The inspector talked to the Dy. SP about this.

Dy. SP listened carefully and said, '"OK, let's go. I'll talk to her."'

"They both came to the police station. Dy. SP took her statement. She said, '"He came at dusk and lay outside. I prepared the dinner and served on the plate, put it on the earth, and covered it with other utensil. After some time, I went to sleep. I don't know what happened after that."'

"Dy. SP said, '"OK. Let's go to the crime scene. They all went to the hut in the evening. Dy. SP said to the wife to prepare dinner and he sent a constable to buy some rice, vegetables, oil, etc. She prepared and put it in the same place and in the same way as on the crime day, as she was ordered. There was total darkness. Not that velvety darkness, but terrible darkness. After three hours, the inspector turned on a torch and they saw the food was covered with red ants. Dy. SP declared that it also happened that day.

"The husband may have drunk, so he couldn't know it, and he had eaten the red ants with food and the poison of the red ants with alcohol killed him. And the police released the wife.

Members of the Fab Four were listening to the story carefully. It was a new thing for them. Colonel Vinod, Hameed, and the children were in a cozy room at a hotel in Alibagh. They came here on a vacation. They had planned to explore the Konkan, particularly the Ratnagiri area. All day they enjoyed Alibagh beach, Kulaba fort, water sports, and Paragliding. Vinod was not with them, as usual, he was indulged in some official work but unofficially, because officially he was on vacation, but he doesn't believe in any vacation, always used to work, that's why other officers called him the work machine. Many people think of their work as worship, but Vinod thinks differently. His work is his hobby, his passion, and because of that, he works 24x7.

Vinod was also in the room, so Arhan asked him, "Uncle, can ants kill a man when eaten?"

Only Arhan has the gut to talk to Vinod. Other trio children always feel tongue-tied before Vinod. Although, he talked to them politely, except Arhan no one dares to talk to him, even his son Vijay couldn't talk to him.

Vinod replied, "There'd be two probabilities. One, as we Indians are a chatterbox, it may be empty chatter only. Another possibility would be that red ants were eaten in ample quantities. But I doubt it. Anyway, if it's a story, I'll say it's a good one. But Hameed tell them about your first case, it was also very interesting." With the reply, Vinod left the room.

Now children surrounded Hameed. "What was the case?" Balwant asked.

"Oh Rubbish, it was like a joke."

"OK, we want to listen to the joke," Said Miss Marple.

"But..." Hameed tried to protest, but everyone insisted on telling the joke. At last, Hameed bowed down to their insistence. He started, "It was my first case. I have arrested a thief. I was happy about my success. I presented him in the court before a magistrate. He was repeating '"I'm innocent."'

"The magistrate asked him for his character certificate. In those days, a character certificate given by a school principal or a reliable person had great value. Not only the social circle, but the police, courts, and government honored it. In courts, it was considered as if the person is good and he may have done the wrong because of some compulsion or circumstance, or else he will be innocent. In that case, he was given a milder punishment than usual.

"So the magistrate asked character certificate, and he said, '"This officer will give my character certificate,"' he said, pointing at me. I got nervous; it was my first chance to face a magistrate. Bestir me, "I said, "I... I don't know him."

"He said to the magistrate, '"What else certificate can I present, sir, I was born here, live here 40 years, and the police don't know me, that means I never ever came to contact with the police, that means I'm a decent gentleman."' The magistrate smiled and let him go scot-free because of his witty argument."

Vijay is an amateur detective; his father Colonel Vinod is also one of the greatest detectives. Once he was called the greatest detective in Asia. At that time, he used to work in the field and now is the police commissioner of Mumbai. Vinod was from a very well affluent family. He doesn't need a job to earn a living; he accepted it only because he loves detection. In those days what he got as a monthly salary, was less than his one day spend.

Vijay wants to be a great detective like him, as it is said, 'like father, like son.' Arhan, Balwant, and Marple are his friends or, to be precise, his teammates in his Passion for detection.

Arhan's father, Captain Sajid Hameed, was the assistant to Colonel Vinod from the very beginning. They shared a very strong bond and were like brothers. Even he lived with Vinod in his grand bungalow. While Vinod was serious by nature, Hameed rarely gets serious; he always used to be in a light mood. Now he is a DCP, under Vinod. Arhan also wants to be a great detective like his father, Captain Hameed.

Balwant is the son of retired army personnel, Colonel Ranjit. Colonel Ranjit was also from the military secret service. He had led many military operations against hostile countries. He used to tell his friends about his dangerous military missions.

And Miss Marple is the daughter of a nurse, Agatha. She was from Kerala, God's own country. She was an Anglo Indian; her mother (The grandmother of Miss Marple) was fond of reading, particularly detective novels by Agatha Christie, that's why she gave her daughter the name Agatha, and later to her granddaughter, Marple, as she was impressed by the famous character of Agatha Christie's novels Miss Marple. Marple is a team member of the Fab four because she is their friend and likes the adventure and excitement of the detection.

They enjoyed the activity in Alibagh, but they didn't like the humid atmosphere there. That's why neither they went out to any recreation in the evening, nor did they let Hameed go. They wanted now full relaxation. Actually, it was not evening; the clock was striking at 9:00 PM.

Vinod returned and was sitting with them. He said, "Before we go for dinner, I tell you a true story. It's not a detective story. Hameed told you about Nevandram, his sister was married to Madhavdas son of Uttamchand. One day that Uttamchand went to the Tahsildar office with a lit-up lantern and said '"It is very dark here; I have come here to spread light."' And it's a true incident that happened in 1949-50. This incident was told to me by his neighbor Mr. Ramratan Sharma alias Kuddu Maharaj."

Now they went to the dining hall of the hotel for dinner except Vinod, who again went somewhere. All the tables were full except a few. The buzzing sound of people talking and the clutter of cutleries echoed throughout the hall.

They sat at a table and get busy checking the menu. After that, they ordered and by the time dinner was served; they started talking. Miss Marple asked, "Uncle, you said the oldest form of clubs. What do you mean by it?"

"Look, as you see today's social clubs. In India, the chaupal is the same as the social clubs. From the very beginning, every village has a chaupal; usually, it is a round platform under an old Papal or Banyan tree, in the center of the village. Every evening people used to sit there, gossiping, talking about village problems and arbitrage. It's a very olden legacy from Vedic times.

"In Vedic times, until they hadn't found the mystery of the fire. They understood the fire but didn't know how to ignite it, so they always kept it lit up in the center of the village. They used to cover it to save it from the rain. And by any chance when a village's fire was extinguished, they borrowed it from another village.

"In those times, the whole village used to cook food in the fire that was the center of the village and eat there like a family. Later they knew how to ignite the fire and slowly from one family to became different families and ignite their fire in their homes and cook and eat food in their respective homes. And they used to sit in chaupal instead of that big fire."

"Oh."

Balwant asked, "Uncle is there a case that you and Colonel couldn't solve and want it to be solved if possible?"

To listen to the topic all the children started listening carefully. Hameed silenced for a few minutes, and then he said, "Yes there are several cases, but one is different in some aspect. That was the case of Thakur Virendra Singh, from Nashik, whose business and residence are here as well. He is a friend of Father Hard Stone. His son was kidnapped, we solved the case, the culprits were arrested, but the boy is not found until today."

"Uncle, please tell us, it seems interesting." it was Vijay.

At that moment, the waiter came and started setting the dinner on the table, so they get silent and indulged in serving themselves. They started their dinner and Hameed took the story forward. "About 25 years back, Thakur Virendra Singh's son was kidnapped. He was from Nashik and a friend of Colonel Vinod. One day, he came here and met Father Hard Stone. He had lodged the complaint at Nashik police station, but he wanted help from Vinod to find his son. He told Colonel, '"My son Suraj, about four years, was in the garden with his nanny. She is an old widowed lady and belonged to Suraj's maternal family. My wife is no more, so she fosterage him. She loves his mother, which means my late wife and Suraj as well, like her son.

'"That day, he was playing ball in the garden. He threw away the ball and his nanny went to bring the ball. When she returned, Suraj was not there. She tried to find him and then came to me and told me about it. We searched around but couldn't find him. I lodged a complaint but in a vain. After being disappointed on all sides, I come to you."' He said with tears in his eyes and a choked throat.

"Colonel said, '"Officially, I can't do anything in the matter, but I'll come with you to Nashik."'

"We trio went to Nashik, around 170 km from Mumbai. There we worked on the case. First, we went to the police station. There, colonel asked the related police inspector about the progress of the case.

"He replied, '"We have tried hard, but in the vain."'

'"Didn't you get any clue?"'

'"No other than a torn slip of paper from the garden. We tried to fix and read it, but most of its letters were blurred and the ink was smeared with moisture from the trees and grass. It was totally illegible."'

"Colonel asked, '"Can I see that slip please?"'

“Oh sure, sure.” He told a constable to bring the Suraj kidnapping case file and ordered another constable to bring some tea and biscuits for Vinod and Hameed.

“Vinod scrutinized the slip with sipping the tea. There were only three words readable, ‘Will,’ ‘name’ and ‘Suraj.’

‘“What did you conclude from this?”’ Vinod asked.”

‘“Actually, I couldn’t understand what it points to.”’

‘“OK,”’ said Vinod, and got ready to leave. He thanked the inspector for his cooperation and they both left the police station and started to Thakur Virendra Singh.

“In the car, Vinod asked me, ‘“What do you think about the slip?”’

“Nothing.”

“At Thakur Virendra Singh’s home, he interrogated everyone. He suspected Thakur Virendra Singh’s younger brother, Dilip Singh. Colonel grilled him and he blurted out the truth. He was living with his brother and dependent on him. He kidnapped Suraj through Randhir Singh, a notorious criminal. Dilip had told Randhir not to kill Suraj, so he must have brought him here to Mumbai and given Suraj to someone.

“And while returning to Nashik, Randhir’s car skidded and fell into a deep gorge at Kasara Ghat and he was killed in the accident.

“We tried hard but couldn’t find Suraj. Even today, Thakur Virendra Singh cries for his memory. He forgave his brother Dilip because he had given his words to his father that he will care for him, and secondly because he felt that his family’s name would be dragged into the mud if his brother was sent to jail. Now Dilip lives with his brother and weeps for his deeds and Suraj. We were not officially on the case, so the colonel let him go.”

Vijay said, “Uncle, suppose we try to find Suraj?”

"How?"

"If you say yes, then we will see how we can do it. Hi friends, what do you say?"

All members of Fab Four said they were ready.

Hameed too said, "You may do it if you want, there is no problem."

So, it's how their first operation started. '**Operation missing boy**.'

2

All teammates met in the park. They had returned from vacation.

"Now where?" asked Arhan.

Vijay said, "I'm going to my college."

"OK, go ahead, but tell me one thing. How can we find that missing boy, if the police and even the great Colonel Vinod couldn't find him?" Balwant asked.

"Yes, I'm also thinking about it," said Miss Marple.

Arhan said, "And how will we recognize him? Now he would be around 30 years. Even his father can't recognize him."

Vijay was smiling, "OK, friends, we shall meet in the evening, and then I'll reply to all your queries."

"How could he do it?" Miss Marple again showed her worry.

Arhan said, "We will know in the evening, as he told us. So don't worry, why should we worry about anything unnecessary?"

They all went to their respective homes.

In the evening, they all met at the park. It was not dusk time, but the sun was about to set, and the light was not so bright. Due to this, the heat had subsided a bit, and the weather had become a bit pleasant. They were sitting on the green grass, and it feels a little cool.

Trio members surrounded Vijay; he was the center of their attention. All have their questions. “Stop it, stop it, stop it, and just give me a chance to clear all things,” Vijay said smilingly.

“When uncle was telling us the story, I was thinking about assistant professor Jay Sharma.”

“What’s the relationship between both?” Balwant asked.

“That’s what I’m trying to tell you. Be patient. So, I was saying that when uncle was telling us the story, assistant Professor Jay Sharma and his father Professor Rajan Sharma strikes in my mind. Some time back I went to their house. Professor Jay Sharma called me to his house. They both are good educationists and very good human beings. He wanted to give me some tips on history.

“When I reached his home, I seated in the hall, they were in the other room. They were talking about Professor Jay’s marriage. Junior Sharma said, ‘“Today, I went to meet Manisha, to fix our marriage, but her father said that he got wind that I’m not your son, so he will not marry Manisha to me. What should I do dad? Am I not your son?”’

“Senior professor said in a shivery voice, ‘“I wanted to tell you this earlier. But every day I thought I’ll tell you tomorrow and time ran like the sand from our hands.”’

‘“Then who are my parents?”’

‘“I don’t know. About 25 years ago, I found you in a park. I tried to find your parents, but all my efforts were in vain. Then I fell in love with you. I couldn’t even imagine being apart from you. For you only, I didn’t marry.”’

‘“I’m not complaining. I know you love me, and I too love you. I least bother about my parents, but I’m in a dilemma now. Manisha’s father says he will not allow Manisha to marry me because my caste is unknown. I love Manisha also. Now what should I do?”’

'"My son if I knew, I certainly would tell you, but I hope we may know who your parents are."'

"So friends, the times of both cases are similar, I think Professor Jay Sharma might be Suraj. That's why I said we can solve the case."

"Now, we have to find the date of the kidnapping of Suraj and the date of the finding of Professor Jay Sharma. As soon as we'll find it, we can match it. If the date is the same, it means that Suraj is Professor Jay Sharma. Simple."

"And how would you find both dates?" Miss Marple asked.

"For Suraj's kidnapping date, we'll meet uncle Hameed and for Jay's finding date we shall meet Professor Rajan Sharma."

Trio members finalized the program and went to their homes.

Vijay, Arhan, Balwant, and Miss Marple were sitting before Captain Hameed, "So, why all of you are here today?"

"Uncle, that day, you told us about the Suraj kidnapping case. Can you please tell us the date of the incident?" Vijay asked.

Hameed looked at everyone. Then he said, "What's the matter? Have you found Suraj? Wow, within one day?" Hameed teased them.

"Oh, no uncle, if we have to work on the case, then we must have all the facts, no?" Balwant said.

"OK. The date, hmm... I don't have a record. Actually, the case was not given to us officially, so we don't have written facts. Now, 25 years have passed, so I forgot. Anyway, I'll ask Thakur Sahib, and then will tell you."

"Suppose we go to talk to him?" Vijay asked.

"Yes, you may. I'll give you his address. Go there and ask whatever you want to know. I'll call him to cooperate with you." Hameed gave him the address written on a piece of paper. He said, "But, we are not in contact, so, at the moment, I don't have a phone no. You go there and call me from there I'll tell him about you."

"OK."

They left.

Out of Hameed's office, they decided that Vijay and Arhan will go to meet Thakur Virendra Singh. Balwant and Miss Marple left for their homes and Vijay and Arhan for Thakur Virendra Singh, on a battery-operated black colour scooter. Vijay was not yet 18 so he can't get a driving license, so he bought this battery operated scooter. To drive it he doesn't need a driving license. Although, it doesn't get a speed over 40, in Mumbai's traffic 40 is OK. And the other thing is something is better than nothing.

They reached Suraj Mansion. It was an enormous mansion. The house was situated at a commanding corner of a road facing the East. It was a noble-looking building. A sculpture of a lion guarded the broad steps leading on either side, each of whom held, in its massive stone paws, a plain shield, inscribed welcome greeting to visitors. Over the portico was designed a scroll that bore the name Suraj Mansion in clearly cut capitals, and the monogram S. M.

They entered and knocked on the door. A middle-aged person opened the door. Vijay asked, "Thakur Virendra Singh."

"No, I'm his unfortunate younger brother, Dilip Singh."

"Why are you calling yourself unfortunate?"

"You will not understand. Anyway brother is not here, he is expected any minute. Can I do something?"

"We came for Suraj's case. Captain Hameed sent us."

He said sadly, “Oh! You were asking why I call myself unfortunate. No? That is the reason. I am the person who is guilty of his kidnapping. I did it, only for the greed of money. Now, my brother has given everything to me, but everything seems to me like a cobra, that bites me every minute. You see, its noon and I’m drinking alcohol. I want to forget everything in booze. But even this can’t help me. I can’t forget Suraj for a minute.” He looked at both of them with a sigh, and then continues, “You know why all this happened?”

Both shrugged their shoulders.

“Only because of greed and inanity, or what should I say? Forget it. It happened because an absurdity entered my mind that my brother is going to give all the property to Suraj, and you know what happened?

They shook their heads.

“After knowing all this villainy, he never said me a single word. It’s eating me up inside. I think why didn’t he kill me? Why didn’t throw me out? Because of me, my nephew... I can’t imagine what’s happening to him, and here I’m enjoying. And you know more?”

They again shook their heads.

“One day he told me, ‘“Dilu, it’s not your fault, not anyone’s fault, it’s entirely my fault. Money blindfolded me; I used to think that money could do anything and everything. I had forgotten that money always has an evil force, and it made you its prey. After snatching my child, Almighty God opened my eyes. I remember that day a person came to me, because I had filed a case against him for recovery and I won the case and get the order to auction his house and recover my money. He came to me for help, to temporarily stop the auction of his house, and all he needed was a temporary respite. He kept on begging for a chance, but I rebuffed him. Maybe it was his curse. He had requested many times that his house should not be auctioned, it is his ancestral home, and he has small children. Where will he go with them? But I didn't listen."'

'"He said to me, '"Kindly, help me and God will bless you."' And I had said it out of arrogance; '"tell him that don't have mercy upon me. I don't need his mercy. Whatever I have, if I protect it carefully then even God could not snatch it from me and I know how to protect my money."'

'"Now I came to know money can't do anything. But I had to pay a heavy price for this knowledge. Now I can't even find my child, what is the use of all of this money? Dilu, take this key and get my will. I want to change it."'

"You know what was in that will, and what was he wanted to change?"

They again shook their heads.

"Half of his property was given to me and a half to Suraj, and I had presumed he would give his entire property to his son Suraj! I had asked in amazement, "Half of the property was in my name?" He said, '"Yes, you are my brother, you have the right, it's your share and you'll get it, but the other half, that's in the name of Suraj, I want to bestow it to the charity of the people."'

'"And I said, "But, brother, my gut feeling said we will find him one day."'

"He said, '"I too think in that way. The God Almighty saw I'm always pursuing money, so He gave me more, more and more money and snatched my son and had given to such a person who needs him, not the money. He, who cares for human beings. Dilu kindly pray for me, I need it badly."'

"I said, '"I'll find him anyhow, and you know what's more?"'

They again shook their heads.

"It happened yesterday and the God Almighty sent you today here. Now I'm sure we will find him." After a moment's silence, he said, "Anyway, tell me, I may help you in the matter."

Before Vijay could say anything, there came a motor sound and Dilip said, "Brother has come."

He went and opened the door. There was Thakur Virendra Singh, in white coloured clothes. He was over 5.6 feet, with fair skin, and a little heavy body. Wasn't shaved for two days and a turban was on the head like old times Rajah.

He looked at Vijay and Arhan questioningly. Dilip said, "Captain Hameed, send them to meet you. They come to talk to you about Suraj."

"Why?"

Vijay replied, "Sir, we are working on the case. We..."

Thakur Virendra Singh didn't give him a chance to say a word, and exploded, "What he thinks about me? If colonel Vinod couldn't find my son, you tiny children can find him? You all are idiots, or do you think I'm an idiot? How dare he insult me? Dilip, call him."

"Sir, sir, I'm the son of Colonel Vinod and this is the son of captain Hameed," said Vijay, putting on a brave smile. "Uncle told me about your predicament, and I offered to assist in the case because they couldn't succeed at the time, but we have enough time to devote our full attention to the case and with your blessing, we may succeed. That's all there is to it. It's not an attempt to bring you down."

Dilip intervened, "Brother, brother, you know yesterday what we were talking about, and the God Almighty sent them today here. I'm sure we will find him, certainly find him. He who sent them here He will give success to them."

"Oh, you are the son of Colonel Vinod and the son of captain Hameed. I know they both are sharp, intelligent, smart, and brave. Yes, you are right, they always have several assignments, so they couldn't dedicate their time and efforts and couldn't focus fully on the case. You are their sons, then I hope you may be like them and may solve the case, what do you want to know?"

"Thanks, sir, for considering us for fit in the case. I want to know the date when the crime was committed?"

"I cannot forget the date of that dreadful misfortune. This was his date of birth when he was kidnapped. That was June 25."

"Thanks, sir. It's enough for the moment. If I need any information or help, I'll call you"

"You are always welcome. But don't call me sir. I am a friend of your father, you can call me uncle. And you won't leave until you take something. Let me be a good host."

"Sir, sorry Uncle, we don't need anything."

"It's OK. But you may take a cup of tea. Shanti, bring some tea for our little guests."

Thakur Virendra Singh didn't leave them until they took some tea and biscuits, although, there were several food items with tea.

3

From Thakur Virendra Singh, they went to meet Professor Rajan Sharma. Professor Rajan Sharma lives in one BHK flat with his son, Jay. The flat next to his flat was also his. His sister lives in that flat, who had come to live with him after his husband's death. She cares for both flats. Vijay pushed the call bell button. Professor Rajan Sharma himself opened the door. Vijay touched his feet respectably.

He said, “Oh, Vijay, how are you?”

“Fine sir, thank you”

“Come in, be seated.”

Vijay and Arhan entered the room and were seated. Professor also seated before them. He said, “Well, is there anything I can do?”

“Sir, first of all, I beg your pardon that last time when I came here, you were talking to your son, and unwantedly, your conversation was coming to my ears. Through that conversation, I came to know that Jay, sir, was not your son. Although it’s not my matter, if you don’t mind, sir, I want to say with your permission, that, can you tell me the date of your finding of him?”

Professor sat silently. Even he couldn’t move. Vijay said, “Sir.”

He was startled, and a tear fell from his eye. He said in a sad voice. “I love him too much. I can’t live without him, but be it as God’s will. If He had prepared my destiny in that way, let it be as His wish.”

“Sir, I don’t want to hurt you, but you yourself know he will not be happy without Manisha and he can’t marry her without knowing of his family.”

He heaved a sigh, “Yes I know. We can’t do anything without His will. What were you asking?”

“Sir, the date of...”

“Yes, the date. It was the 25th of June. I celebrate it as his birth date. I was in the park near to my home and those days I lived in another locality. I found him under a bench. I was a school teacher then and with his luck, not only I got this job as a professor in the college, but bought a flat in this locality.

“The sun was setting, and it was twilight or say golden dark. The soft gentle breeze felt pleasant, as you know in the month of June days are hot and humid. But in the park, the cool breeze was pleasurable. I was sitting on a bench enjoying the atmosphere and was thinking something, and suddenly there came a child's cry. I was startled and looked around, but no one was there. The cry came again, and I felt it was coming under the bench. I looked down. A child, about 4-5 years was there in expensive attire. I saw around to find someone to whom the child belongs. But summarily I understood that someone deliberately left the child. The clothes could show that he belongs to a wealthy family. They must have ruined financially and couldn't be able to nurture the child.

"I brought him home. That child is Asst. Professor Jay Sharma. I didn't marry, because of him. I think, if he didn't come into my life, how would be my life, full of gloom and misery. But... Anyway, forget it."

"Sir, why don't you think that if you didn't come into his life, how would be his life?"

Professor said nothing, he kept quiet.

"Sir, do you have the clothes, he wore at the time when you got him?"

He nodded, "Yes, I have those clothes, kept carefully. And with clothes, there was some jewelry and talisman all things are kept carefully."

Vijay asked, "Where is he now?"

"I don't know," he sobbed. "I don't know where he has gone. He didn't tell anybody, not even me. He simply submitted a leave application and left. Because Manisha's parents oppose her marrying him."

"Oh. Sir my father is the Commissioner of the police. If you like, I'll talk to him."

"I know about your father, Colonel Vinod, the great detective. OK, do whatever you can."

"Thanks, sir. Can you tell me about him in detail?"

"I have told you all about him."

"I mean, about Manisha's parents?"

"Actually, they have chosen a boy for her. She was a fan of Jay's poetry. That appreciation grew into love and she now wants to marry him. He too loves her. I don't know any other detail."

"OK, I'll do my best."

"Thanks."

"Welcome sir." Vijay further asked, "Sir, may I ask one more question? It's about you, sir."

"What?"

"Sir, would you feel bad or, I should say, would you feel downcast if his parents are found?"

"Now it doesn't matter. If he'll feel happy, I'll be happy in his joy."

"Sorry to hurt you, sir, but I have to find his father."

"That's good, I'm happy to listen to this," and tears pour down from his eyes. But Vijay or Arhan couldn't see this.

Now the matter had taken a new turn. Instead of Professor Jai Sharma's paternity, Vijay had to find Professor Sharma first. From there, Vijay wanted to meet Manisha's parents. But it was a sensitive matter, so he asked Balwant's father, Colonel Ranjit's help. Vijay told him everything about Professor Jay Sharma, except for the relationship with Thakur Virendra Singh. He easily got ready. He said, "It is a virtue to unite two lovers. I'll do everything for that."

He went to meet Manisha's father with Vijay and asked him about Asst. Professor Jay Sharma and Manisha. Her father said, "I'm Manisha's father. Worrying about her future is my duty. If she marries him, not only she, but my whole family will suffer. I have chosen a suitable boy for her. He is well-educated, good-looking, and from a wealthy family, but she said he is very old-fashioned and always gives his opinion on every matter. She doesn't like that.

"Actually, he is just a bit conservative. He belongs to Banaras, so his mentality; the way of thinking is like townsfolk, if he lived here for some time he will be changed. But suppose when he says we should take a little less sugar, so what's bad in that? After all, I'm doing it all for her own good."

"OK, but do you know that Professor Sharma is missing?"

"Oh, I'm not aware of it. I would be happy if I could do something for them."

Colonel Ranjit returned from there disappointed, they could not find any clue there. Then they met Manisha and talk to her about Professor Jay Sharma and his disappearance.

Manisha trembled to hear this. She said, "I don't know anything about this. For some time Jay didn't come to meet me, I thought he may be busy somewhere. I too was busy with my job, so I didn't even notice it."

"Has he done this before?"

"Yes, several times he did not come for 4-5 days or sometimes even for a week."

"What is the problem with your father? Why doesn't he like him?"

"That old-fashioned thought."

"But your father says he did this for your happiness."

"Yes, he doesn't like Jay's coming to our home, it is for my happiness, and he wants to marry me with that silly fellow, it is also for my happiness, and I have to bear all these injustices silently, it is also for my happiness, actually they are torturing me in the guise of my happiness."

"How did you come close to him?"

"I'm a singer. My family is wealthy. I don't need to sing for my bread and butter. But I love it, so I sing on the radio and on stage. I sang lyrics from many poets. I came to know about his lyrics, I liked them, had sung them, in that way we came too close, and then we decided to get married."

"OK. Now, can you help us find him?"

"Of course, whatever is necessary, I certainly will do."

Vijay was also there, now he intervened, "I think, as you said you sing on the radio, he certainly used to listen to your programs, no?"

"Yes, he may be."

"OK, do you used to say something before or after the song?"

"Yes, sometimes I describe the song."

"I suggest that tomorrow when you sing on the radio, choose a lyrics by Jay sir, say something about Jay sir and if you like to, say about yourself, and his disappearance and that his parents are found and now your parents are ready to your wedding with him. I'm sure he must listen to your singing and he certainly will return home."

Colonel Ranjit said, "Yes, it's a good idea!"

Manisha agreed as well and the next day she did as suggested and really Jay listened to that program and the same day he called Manisha and asked who his parents were.

Manisha told him she didn't know, but an investigator, Vijay, knows it. And after two days, he returned to his home.

4

Jayant is an assistant manager at Bombay transport. He is slim, 5.6 feet, with fair skin, and a plain middle-class clerk-type person. Thakur Virendra Singh called him, "Jayant, a small transport company in Nagpur named Nag roads is looking to sell their enterprise. If we can buy it, our business could be better in that area as well. We are interested in buying it. They demanded some money in exchange for the dealing. They will adjust it at the time of full payment, but they want one million cash at the moment. If you can go with the cash, we can get the dealing."

"OK, sir, as you say, I'm ready. When should I have to go?"

"Tomorrow will be better. Arrange a ticket for the train, air, bus whatever you can get, even a cab is OK, in case you can't get a reservation. There, meet the owner, Mr. Agrawal. He asks 5.1 million for their several trucks, offices in cities and towns, and their goodwill. Try to bargain it up to 4.5 million, or call me from there. I'll try to bargain on the phone or whatever I can. Now go to your home and get ready."

"Yes, sir."

"I'll send money in the evening to your house."

"Right, sir."

Jayant reached Nagpur and stayed in the Hotel Continental at Central avenue road, near Nagpur railway station. At the reception, he asked about the hotel's vault service. He doesn't want to keep cash in his hotel room, it may be risky. The receptionist told him they have a vault service; he can deposit anything there. He submitted the suitcase to deposit. It was deposited and a receipt was given to him.

He deposited it because today was Saturday and 13th and Thakur Virendra Singh was a little superstitious, he strictly told Jayant to don't deal on Saturday the 13th. Actually, he even didn't like his reaching Nagpur on Saturday, but he thought that he was starting from Mumbai on Friday, so it will be OK; it was OK in his opinion. The next day was Sunday, so the dealing was not possible. That's why he deposited the money in the hotel's vault because keeping such a large amount in the room was stupidity in his eyes.

A bellboy fetched his other belongings to his room. There was a girl seated in the hall at a table near reception. She was in pants and a T-shirt, without any make-up and she looks pretty without any make-up. All his activity was watched by this girl, Kamala. In half an hour Jayant returned to the reception and asked about some recreational activities in the city.

Clerk said, "There is no special activity today. If you like boating, then you may go to Ambazari Lake, around 6 KM from here. You will like it."

Jayant said "OK."

The clerk told him that the hotel can provide him with a car to go there. He said no thanks. Because he knows nothing is free in this world. The hotel may charge double the market rate. The other thing was hotel bill will be borne by the company and this was his personal ride, so he preferred to get a taxi or auto rickshaw from the road.

Within an hour he reached Ambazari Lake. The water was not crystal clear. The surrounding also was not beautiful, but he didn't care, he went boating, and chooses a row boat for one hour. He held the oars in his hand. Before starting he had to wear a life jacket.

After 15 minutes, he was rowing it fast, suddenly a row boat came into his path and his boat hit that boat in the middle and that boat capsized.

A young girl was alone in the boat. She fell into the water. She also wore a life jacket like him. As she was moving her arms and legs, Jayant understood she could not swim. There was no risk of her drowning. She started moving her arms and legs in a panic. He jumped into the water and swam towards her. Then he saw a water snake coming towards the boats. He quickly stretched out his hand and pulled the girl and took her onto his boat, and then he too jumped into his boat.

She was just panicked, otherwise, she was alright. He asked her, "Don't worry, you are safe now. Where do you live?"

She said in a faint voice, "Hotel Continental."

"Oh, what a coincidence! I'm also staying there. I'll leave you there."

He took the boat back to the shore. There, he told the boatmen what happened to her boat and took her to an auto rickshaw.

They reached the hotel where he brings her to his room. At first, he thought about bringing her to her room, but she was still in the accident's trauma and was trembling. He lays her on the bed and ordered some hot milk with bourn Vita. In a few minutes, a server brought the milk. Jayant had her drink the milk. She recovered in a while. She then expressed her regret for her stupidity, which caused the accident.

Jayant said, "It's OK, forget it."

"Now I'm fine. I should go to my room. Papa would worry for me."

"OK. I come with you and tell him what happened."

"No, no, please don't. I don't want to tell him about this, otherwise, he will be strict about my going anywhere."

"OK, as you wish."

"Thanks."

"Can I invite you for the dinner tonight?"

"No, not today. I'll rest in my room and will get something light into the room."

"Oh," he said in despair, and then asked, "What about tomorrow?"

"Tomorrow morning, papa will go to Gondia, a city about 150 KM from here."

"And you?"

"I'll be here. He is going for some business dealings."

"Tomorrow, I'm also free. Can we go somewhere to enjoy?"

"Where?

"I don't know. I'm new here. We may inquire at the reception."

"OK. Will see tomorrow, but don't you think there is a peculiarity about our meeting and your invitation?"

"No, what's it?"

"You invited me, but you don't even know my name, she smiled."

"Oh, oh, I really am a stupid fellow. My name is Jayant."

"I'm Kamala. Good night."

"Good night."

The next morning, Kamala's papa went away in a hired car and Jayant called Kamala from the room phone.

Kamala received the phone and Jayant said, "Hello, good morning, it's Jayant."

"Good morning, Kamala here."

"What's the program today?"

"Look, I inquired at reception and was told that around 50 KM from here, there is an old, small town, Ramtek. There is a centuries-old temple, a giant lake, and interestingly it's the place where Kalidas wrote the Meghdootam, a Sanskrit epic about a loving couple."

"I am not interested in any lake now, but can visit the temple and see the place of Kalidas"

"Why not interested in the lake?"

"After the accident of yesterday, I'm afraid of water."

"But I'll be with you."

"Okay let's go."

Jayant also hired a car, and they went to Ramtek. On the way, Jayant told her about why he came to Nagpur and also revealed that he has one million Rs. with him. But she said, "I'm not interested in the dry subject like business and money."

The driver, Abdul, asked, "Sir, is it your first visit to the Ramtek?"

"Yes," Jayant replied.

"OK, shall I tell you about it?"

"Sure. It would be the icing on the cake."

Abdul started, "This highway goes to Mansar and further to Jabalpur. Mansar has some historical Buddha idols. You may go there if you like."

"No, forget it."

"Then, before Mansar, we will turn to the right. From there you will see the real Ramtek. I mean, there still are old-styled houses and shops and greenery. Ramtek is situated on Ramgiri hill. In the monsoon, this entire area looks so beautiful. That's why the description of nature is so beautiful in Meghdootam by Kalidas because it was written here. And it is said that the Amravati city in the Meghdootam is today's Amravati, which is a very old city about 150 KM from here. And it's also believed that Tulsidas had described Ram, Sita, and Laxman's exile, while staying at Ramgiri Mountain, which is why it has so much beauty in the description.

Jayant and Kamala really liked the road to Ramtek. They had to drive three to four kilometers from the foothill of the hill to the top. There was a parking lot, and Abdul informed them that they can alight there or if they like he can drop them off by the car a little higher. From there they will not have to climb many stairs.

"It's OK," Jayant remarked, "we came here to see everything, so we'd rather walk than drive."

There was a way to climb and two minutes away there were shops of worship materials, toys, tea, snacks etc. Jayant buy a plate full of worship material and went further. The shopkeeper didn't even take the price of the plate or the worship material. He said you may give at returning. They also took off their footwear there. In Hindu and Muslim traditions too, one goes to the place of worship only after taking off the footwear. In two-three minutes they reach the gate of the fortress, in which the temples are situated.

They began by approaching the sculpture of a boar. Someone there informed them that if they passed beneath the boar, they would be free of the bondage of birth and death, and they will get salvation. Jayant did not attempt to pass beneath it, but Kamala did. After it, they proceeded, first to the Hanuman temple, then to the Sita temple, and finally to the Ram temple. There were a lot of monkeys and Langurs. People told them that these monkeys snatch things from tourists, particularly food items, but they didn't do any harm to Jayant and Kamala, even though Kamala was scared of them.

There was a very deep and steep valley near the last temple. They took some photos here from their mobiles. It was windy here. Jayant saw Kamala whose black thick hair was blowing in the wind and Jayant felt as if black clouds were flying in the air. After returning, Jayant paid the price of the worship material and wore their foot wears and returned to their car.

From there they went to Khindasi Lake because the driver told them it was too beautiful. He said, "Although it's a lake, its waves look like the waves of the sea."

There they didn't go for boating, only watch the lake and spent a good time, and then they returned to the town where they get lunch. Abdul told them they may try some local dishes, and on his suggestions, they ordered local foods, and enjoy them. After lunch, they returned to the hotel because her papa told her he will return in the evening.

The next day, Jayant got his money from the hotel vault and get ready for going to the dealing. He called 2-3 times to Mr. Agrawal, but the call didn't connect. He thought that he should phone Mr. Agrawal first before going to meet him. Once more, he called Mr. Agrawal, and this time he got a response. Mr. Agrawal said that he couldn't come to the office now; he will be late so the dealing would be in the evening. Jayant said, "Oh, OK, as you wish."

Mr. Agrawal said, "I'm sorry, but for some personal problems I couldn't come. I'm terribly sorry."

Jayant said, "No problem sir, good day, and we will meet in the evening."

After putting the receiver on the cradle, he started thinking, now what should he do? Should he redeposit the money in the hotel vault? If he put the money in the room, then he couldn't go anywhere, whereas he wanted to go somewhere with Kamala. He met her only two days ago, but he feels as if he knows her for decades. He has fallen for her!

He was thinking about Kamala and there was a knock on the door. He opened the door; it was Kamala at the door. He turned aside to let her in. She entered and saw the suitcase on the table containing money and said, "Papa went to the market, what's your program?"

"I had to go for a business meeting, but it is just canceled and you came here, I was thinking, what to do?"

"Hmm... OK, order some tea, and think while you sipping it."

"Oh, sure" and he ordered the room service for tea.

Within minutes a server put the tea on the table and asked, "Sir, do you want anything else?"

"No, not now. I'll let you know later."

Kamala asked Jayant, "Do you have some biscuits?"

"Yes, of course," he said and went to the cabinet for biscuits.

As he turned to the cabinet, Kamala gently dropped something into his cup. He came back with some biscuits and put them on the table. Kamala took one and talked to him while nibbling it and sipping the tea. A few minutes after finishing the tea, Jayant held his head with both hands and said, "Oh, my head is dizzying."

"Oh, what happened? Please come with me and lie down on the bed. I think you will be right in minutes." Kamala supported him and took him to the bed and made him lie down. She took his hand in her hands. He lies down and lost consciousness in no time.

As he got unconscious she dialed a number and said, "OK, The work is done."

In a minute his father appeared with a suitcase. They opened Jayant's suitcase and put all the money in their suitcase. They took the suitcase and went out of the room. She closed the door from outside but before going out they wiped their fingerprints from everywhere. But they forgot that Kamala's photos were on Jayant's mobile.

When Jayant got up, his head was still dizzy. Kamala was not there, the suitcase was on the table as was earlier. He breathed a sigh of contentment at the sight of it. He called reception and asked for a doctor. Within half an hour, the receptionist came to his room with a doctor. The doctor checked him. He told him that after taking tea his head started dizzying and later he was lost in sleep. Then he said to the doctor, "Doctor, I ask you one more favor. Please deposit this suitcase in the hotel vault for me."

The doctor said, "OK, you don't worry, get rest."

And at the same time, the receptionist said, "but your suitcase is open."

Jayant woke up with a jolt. The receptionist picked up the handle of the suitcase and said shockingly, "Hey, it's empty."

"What?" Jayant was amazed.

"Yes, it's empty."

Jayant immediately got up and opened it and was shocked to see it empty.

The doctor asked, "What was in the suitcase?"

"One million rupees," Jayant said.

"Oh," the doctor said, "Now I got it. Someone has duped you. Now you rest a little and you will be better. There was some intoxicant mixed in the tea. Its effect will go away gradually."

Jayant was silently seated on his bed. Then he called Thakur Virendra Singh with his mobile and told him all the matter and asked what to do. Thakur sahib said, "Don't lodge a complaint, because I don't want to disclose about the dealing. You come here then we will think what to do."

"OK."

The receptionist was listening to this, he said, "Sir, the father-daughter duo checked in only a few minutes before you, and a little while ago they checked out. It does mean they knew about you and your money and your program."

Jayant said nothing. He lay down and was thinking. What should he do? Although Thakur sahib told him to come here, he knows now he will not be trusted by him. He always will be viewed with suspicion. He had Kamala's address and photos. He decided he will go to her and get the money returned.

And he was right in one matter. When he called Thakur Virendra Singh, Manvendra Singh was also there and he asked, "What's the matter?"

Thakur sahib told him all and Manvendra Singh gave his opinion, "can't it be possible that Jayant has embezzled the money and is telling the incorrect news?"

Thakur Virendra Singh said, "He is an honest boy, but every man's honesty has a price tag. When and at how much money made a man dishonest can't be said."

5

Today was Jay's wedding with Manisha. Colonel Vinod, Captain Hameed, and the Fab Four members were invited. Thakur Virendra Singh himself had come to invite them all. He told them that Professor Rajan Sharma also lives with them and now Jay got two fathers and both fathers were happy. He insisted on joining the wedding. That's why all were presented. But they didn't know that this time will turn into a mourning time!

Beautiful electric lights decorated the entire house and lawn. The beautiful house attached to the lawn was thrown open and lavishly decorated with flowers, fountains, and twinkling lights; an awning extended from its windows right down the avenue of dark trees, which were ornamented with lights; and the entire house was en fete. Intricate patterns of gold and silver were adorned on the walls, and the floor was covered in a soft white carpet. The stage was decorated with a large, white cloth draped over it, and a beautiful flower garland in the shape of two hearts was hanging from the ceiling. The tables and chairs were elegantly decorated with white clothes and beautiful floral centerpieces. Soft music was playing in the background, and the entire hall was filled with a warm and inviting atmosphere.

But the wedding place was in a cruiser. It was Dilip's idea. He booked a cruiser for the purpose. Thakur Virendra Singh and other family members entered into his plans with spirit; and, what was far more important, Thakur Virendra Singh opened his purse readily to every demand for the necessary or unnecessary, every type of expense. So nothing was stinted; an elegant dinner was laid out in the large dining hall. The delicious strains of a band floated to the ears as the guests descended the staircase on their way to the scene of celebrations; and suggestions of fairyland were presented in the graceful girlish forms, clad in light, almost transparent attire, that flitted here and there, or occasionally passed them.

A wealth of the purest white flowers decorated it, mingling their delicious fragrance with the faintly perceptible fragrance of incense. On all sides of the cruiser, there were lights, and everywhere was incense burning like fireflies in twilight. It was Professor Rajan Sharma's idea. He said instead of synthetic room fresheners they can use incense that would appeal to the people. A stage was set up in a corner; laid a wreath of magnificent crimson roses. It would seem as though some high festival were about to be celebrated, and guests gazed around with beating hearts, half expecting some invisible touch to awaken the notes of the organ and a chorus of spirit voices!

The plan was that the cruiser would leave the port at 8:00 PM and the guests arriving later would reach the cruiser by motor boats. A seaplane was also hired for the groom and the bride and their parents for the wedding. At the time of the wedding, the plane would be in the air means the wedding would be in the sky, and after the wedding, it would land in the sea and they all will reach the cruiser by boat. After that, the bride and the groom will be on the stage and guests will enjoy their dinner.

Vinod and Hameed and the Fab Four arrived at the pier by car; from there they were taken to the cruiser. When Vijay reach the wedding site, Dilip was at the entry door, made of flowers, welcoming the guests. He was looking sober and happy. He welcomes Vijay and told him that he had given up the habit of boozing; now he is very happy and after Jay's wedding he too was planning to marry. He said, "I have even chosen a girl, Chandrika, she is the daughter of Manvendra Singh, our transport business manager. Both the father and daughter have come into the marriage, I'll show you." He was glistening with joy.

After meeting him, Vijay moved ahead to meet Thakur Virendra Singh, Suraj, Manisha, and Professor Rajan Sharma. After some time, he saw Dilip going somewhere. Vinod and Hameed were busy meeting people. Fab Four members were going from this food stall to that food stall and test all the food items.

Later suddenly an aged person started crying, "My daughter, my daughter, Dilip killed my daughter. Thakur Virendra Singh came near him and asked, "Manvendra, what happened?"

"Sir, Dilip killed my daughter."

"Dilip? It's not possible."

"Sir, I am not lying. Come with me and see for yourself."

Thakur Virendra Singh, Colonel Vinod, captain Hameed, Vijay, and some other people went with him.

Vinod stops everyone from entering Dilip's cabin. Vinod and Hameed entered the cabin. In the cabin Dilip was seated on a sofa chair, pressing his head with his hands, like he was in a pain. In his clothes and two-three other places, blood was splattered. Dilip was also bathed in blood, and there was a strong smell of alcohol coming from Dilip.

Vinod said Hameed to call the police, homicide, forensic department, and medical to come to the crime scene. Hameed got busy with the calls on his mobile, although the signals were weak. The Wi-Fi of the cruiser was good, so he WhatsApp-called everyone. Vinod had completed the investigation. Now he was interrogating Dilip. Dilip said, "I came here to find Chandrika because she told me she was going to use my cabin to be ready for the wedding. Mr. Manvendra was with her, but he returned to the function. She asked me about Suraj, how he was kidnapped, etc. And I told her the truth, and suddenly she started shouting, she said don't try to meet me again; she said I don't want to meet a criminal who kidnapped his own nephew. I got angry too and as I was going to slap her, something hit me on the back side of my head and I fell unconscious. I don't know what happened after that."

Vinod asked Manvendra what happened, he said, "I was coming to the cabin to see why Chandrika is getting late because it was late to join the function. When I came near to the cabin I heard the voices of Chandrika and Dilip as if they were having a heated argument. I quickly headed to the cabin to see what was going on. When I reach the cabin Chandrika was on the floor covered in blood and Dilip was seated on the sofa chair, a blood-stained knife in his hand, and he couldn't sit properly because of the booze I think." He said, crying, "He killed my daughter."

But where is the dead body? Neither Dilip nor Manvendra could tell it. Vinod ordered the police to search for the body in the sea. He had seen a window in the cabin that could be used to throw away the body. The police had searched within a two-kilometer radius, but couldn't find the body. The next day, Vinod was informed about it.

Vinod also sent Dilip to custody, Thakur Virendra Singh said, "My brother can't murder the girl, whom he loves." He said to Vinod, "You know he even didn't kill Suraj. I couldn't believe that he committed the murder of his love."

Vinod said dryly, "Sorry, but I can't help you. I can understand your point, but the evidence is against him. I have to arrest Dilip."

Police arrested Dilip and fetch him to the police station. Vinod and Hameed also returned from the wedding along with Fab Four. Vinod said to Hameed before leaving, "Follow me, I'll stop at some restaurant, there we will get some food because here I couldn't eat dinner."

From returning Vijay was with Vinod and the others were with Hameed.

Vijay said, "I can't imagine Dilip as a murderer."

"Many times, the truth is stranger than the imagination. If you think he didn't kill Suraj, so couldn't kill anybody, then you must consider Suraj was blood-related to him. That's why he may show some mercy, it doesn't mean he may show compassion on everyone."

Vijay didn't dare to say anything else before Colonel Vinod.

Vinod stopped the car in front of a small restaurant. After him, Hameed also stopped his car, and all entered the restaurant. There, they all ate food reluctantly. Everyone was thinking about Dilip. After dinner, they returned to their homes.

6

The next day, Hameed was seated before Vinod in his cabin. Vinod was thinking, and a lighted cigar was in his hand. He said in deep thought, “I know Dilip is innocent and trapped by someone.”

“If you know he is innocent, then why did you arrest him?”

“It was a tactic. If he wasn’t arrested, he can be implicated in some other case.”

“Oh.”

“Now listen. Close monitor for everyone involved with him and his family.”

“OK. I will put some cops into this case.”

“Good. Give me a report periodically.”

Fab Four were also in a meeting. They were sitting in a park. Vijay was saying, “Look, what uncle Virendra Singh said, I too agree with him. Dilip couldn’t be the murderer. Yesterday, when he was telling about Chandrika, he looked so gleeful, and his eyes were full of adoration. Dilip must be framed by someone. We must find that culprit.”

Other trio said in chorus, “Yes, you are right.”

Arhan said, “I think we should meet Uncle Virendra Singh. After talking to him, we may get a clue.”

Balwant said, “Not only Uncle Virendra Singh but Suraj, Professor Rajan Sharma, and Manvendra Singh as well.”

Vijay said, “Yes, but we will start with Uncle Virendra Singh. Last time I went there with Arhan, so this time too will go with him. Thakur Virendra Singh knows him as well, so talking with him will be easy instead with someone else.”

It was decided and Vijay started for Thakur Virendra Singh with Arhan, on his battery-operated black colour scooter. They reach there and met Thakur Virendra Singh. He was seated in despair. To see them, his sadness subsided. He said, "Oh, thank God, He has sent you to me. I was almost anxious with the strain on my nerves and abandoned myself to despair, and this awful incident meant bereavement to me. I thought my last hour had surely come! Then I saw you, and some superhuman instinct in me leaped to life in some strange way. I thought I knew or guessed the horror of what that next utterance would be, and what I say, you know what happened. Only you are the ray of hope to me."

Vijay said, "Uncle, we will do whatever we can."

Thakur Virendra Singh shakes hands in helplessness, "See."

Vijay tried to talk to Thakur Virendra Singh but in vain. He was in a state of desperation, fear of defaming the reputation of his family. A little later Manvendra Singh entered the house. Vijay never imagined that he'll come to the house. Then he thought after all he was an employee of Thakur Virendra Singh, he may come to talk about a business purpose. But he was shocked when Manvendra Singh said, "Thakur sahib, sorry I overreacted yester night. I was in a rage after seeing my daughter's blood and thought of her... But later, I thought, you are right; although I saw the blood-stained knife in Dilip's hand he could not murder his love."

"You are right. If I was in your place, I too would have reacted the same. I'm not angry with you. Even though I hope you think that Dilip didn't commit the murder, then other people will also think that way. Now I'm relieved."

"What did you say about the altercation between Dilip and Chandrika?" Vijay asked.

"Altercation between Dilip and Chandrika doesn't mean he killed her. Now and then we quarrel with this and that fellow. It doesn't mean we kill that fellow."

Then a WhatsApp message came to Thakur Virendra Singh's mobile, 'I know your brother is innocent. If you want details, meet me at Gorai beach at 5 PM. For safety reasons, come via Borivali railway station by ferry and auto rickshaw. Wherever I feel safe, I'll meet you. If I could not meet you on the way, when you reach Gorai beach, turn to the right. After 300 meters, you'll see three palm trees at a place. Wait there. I'll try to meet you there. I want to talk to you, but here the signals are too weak and we can't talk on every matter over the phone. In some cases, it is necessary to talk face-to-face. I'm under the obligation of your family. That's why I want to help you. Please be careful, there are foes in the guise of friends.'

Manvendra Singh said, "Who he would be?"

Thakur Virendra Singh said, "Whoever he will be, for me, he is a God. I certainly would go to meet him."

Vijay said, "Uncle, it may be a decoy for you. Let me go there instead of you."

"Hmm..."

Manvendra Singh said, "But how he will recognize you and meet you? He may know Thakur sahib, so he can meet him."

"You are right, uncle, please send him a message that instead of you I am going there. After meeting him, we can decide it is a decoy or a good deed."

Thakur Virendra Singh said, "OK, as you wish."

Thakur Virendra Singh sent a WhatsApp message, 'I can't come myself, and so I'm sending my nephew Vijay. He is my trusted boy, about 17 years. He will come with a red t-shirt and a white cap. You will recognize him. Meet him and tell him whatever you want to.'

A few minutes later a message came, 'OK, I'll wait for him.'

Manvendra Singh said, "We can trace the person through mobile no."

Thakur Virendra Singh said, "I'm not interested. Vijay my child, go there and leave Arhan here. When you come back, you can fetch him with you to his home. Is it OK?"

"Right uncle, I'm leaving for Gorai. I think it will take over two hours to reach there. It's about 1.30 PM."

Arhan said, "Why can't I too go with Vijay?"

Thakur Virendra Singh said, "No, no, wait, lunch is ready. Go after lunch. And Manvendra you too take lunch here." And he turned to Arhan and said, "There are two reasons. First I told him that Vijay is coming, and if you would be with Vijay, he might get suspicious and shall not meet Vijay. The other reason is I want to talk to you, OK?"

Manvendra Singh said, "Sorry sir, but I have to go to the office."

Thakur Virendra Singh said, "OK, as you like."

Manvendra Singh left and they went to the dining room.

Thakur Virendra Singh's transport business, Bombay transport, is one of the biggest in volume and widest in the network. His rival transport company Nashik transport is second in every manner. Although it's second, the business is less than 50% compared to Bombay transport.

In the office of Nashik transport, a phone call came and asked for general manager Dharmendra Singh. The receptionist connected the call. On the other end said, "Someone is betraying us. He is to meet Vijay at Gorai around 5 PM. Send some hooligans there to fix the problem. At Gorai, the right side has three palm trees in one place. They may meet there or they may meet between Borivali railway station to the meeting place. Do fast, whatever is possible."

General Manager Dharmendra Singh has relations with local goons' leader Ramlal and his daughter Kamala. He ordered him to do whatever was needed.

Around 2.00 PM, Vijay left for Gorai. Thakur Virendra Singh and Arhan were seated in the drawing room. The butler served them coffee there. With sipping coffee, both indulged in gossiping. Thakur Virendra Singh said, "Colonel Vinod is the greatest detective. What do you know about him?"

"Not too much. He is not only a good detective but a good person in many aspects as well. He is an authority on dogs, snakes, medicines, herbs, poisons, and you may say he is a moving encyclopedia on these subjects."

"You like him too much?"

"Yes. The other reason to love him is he also loves me too much."

"Oh, really?"

"Yes, when I was just a kid, I used to stroll with him. He used to take me to the railway track, and sand piles and even he jumps from there and told me to jump from the hill. I too did it and enjoyed it too much. He used to hold Banyan's hair and hang with it and hang me as well."

"Oh, that means he loves you toooo much."

"Yes, and then I used to watch 'Chhota Bheem' a TV program for children, I was obsessed with this program and whenever I had to go through a narrow path, I used to shout "enter the cave," and he too shouts same, he never cared, what the other people will think about him. I'll say in one word, He is Unique!"

Vijay reached Borivali station. He came out to the road. There were autos in line. He went to the first auto and asked for the ferry station to Gorai beach. The driver said, "OK. Sit."

Within minutes, the auto reached out of the city, a single road was going through the greenery, and Vijay was overwhelmed to look both sides but there was a foul smell of the stagnant seawater in the air. He has never seen such a beautiful road in Mumbai. The auto reached the ferry station. He left the auto then paid the fare for the ferry, which was a mere 15 Rs. and boarded the ferry which crosses the creek which is very wide like a big river. Many people were boarded with their two-wheelers. This way they save time, money, and energy, otherwise, they have to go a long way.

Within minutes the ferry crossed the creek. He alighted and got another auto-rickshaw to go to the beach. There was also a beautiful road on this side of the creek, and the foul smell of stagnant seawater was also floating in the air along with the greenery.

Gorai Beach is one of the most serene beaches on the outskirts of Mumbai, with beach resorts, holiday cottages, and home stays. The presence of palm trees and the absence of noisy crowds make it an ideal day trip away from Mumbai.

Gorai beach is also popular among party lovers and adventure seekers. The surrounding resorts have some of the craziest beach parties in the evenings. And water sports make it a fun place during the day. People enjoy here boat rides in the sea and horse riding on the beach and jet skiing, kite surfing, and other sports available at the venue.

One can explore the beach by getting on horseback or camel and riding down the length of the beach. A bullock cart ride to Gorai Beach is also fun to explore the beach with your group.

And walking along the waves with your loved ones, and feeling the cool breeze, can be refreshing. Walk barefoot on the sand or lie down in the shade of a tree, do whatever you want. Also, do not forget to capture beautiful memories with your camera on the picturesque blue-green landscape of the beach.

Gorai Beach New Year Parties are known for loud music, drinking, and all-night-long fun. But the resorts host other parties too, especially on full moon nights. You can sit around the bonfire, sing along with your group and enjoy a hearty meal on a cozy evening. Special beach parties are also organized during the festival of Holi.

The evening is the best time to visit Gorai Beach. It is also known for its beautiful sunset views. When you are at Gorai Beach at night, especially during the full moon nights, it can be a pleasant experience and one can stay overnight in Gorai. It offers good food also, whether you like the street food stalls on the beach or at the food joints around the area. Nearby is Essel World, and with this, you are all set for a perfect weekend getaway.

One can explore the Koli community and their villages, and even discovering old-style homes with old-fashioned charm is fun. Right on the beach, there are several stands selling all kinds of snacks and fresh fruit to keep you going.

Even though, Vijay arrived there in the evening, but he lacked the time and mindset to enjoy all this. He reached Gorai beach and then the place mentioned by the unknown caller. There was no one. He didn't know that the gang of Ramlal was already there and monitoring the place, although he saw some people here and there.

Vijay has no option but to wait there. He was looking around and someone put a hand on his back. He twirled. There was a slim, 5.6 feet, with fair skin, and plain middle-class clerk-type person. He said, "I'm Jayant..." And suddenly blackness descended upon Vijay's eyes; the blow that hit on his head was so powerful. He had gone completely unconscious.

Actually, before Vijay, the hooligans sent by Dharmendra reached Gorai beach and found the place where Vijay was to meet the fellow. They don't know who he may be, so their boss Ramlal left two men at Borivali station so that they could follow Vijay and catch the person who tries to meet Vijay. It's because they did not know the person, but they recognize Vijay. They followed Vijay all the way but he couldn't make out that he is followed; because there were several people going to the ferry station, then the ferry, and then to Gorai beach.

At Gorai, Ramlal saw two-three persons around the spot. He went to them, show them a revolver, and said there would be a police encounter, get away from here as soon as possible and don't tell anyone about it, and they slipped from there as was said and Ramlal did his job to made Vijay unconsciousness and captivate Jayant.

Goons brought Jayant's unconscious body to Ramlal's home. They put him on a bed and Ramlal ordered her daughter Kamala to monitor him. Then they went out.

When Vijay gained consciousness, there was no Jayant. He understood that the goons have taken away Jayant after he fell unconscious. His head ached like a sore. He stood up and walked with heavy steps. He started for Thakur Virendra Singh. In one and a half hours, he was before Thakur Virendra Singh and giving his report. Thakur Virendra Singh said, "Oh my God, are you OK?"

He checked Vijay's head where there was a bump emerged on the right side.

Vijay said, "It's OK." And when he took Jayant's name Thakur Virendra Singh was startled.

He asked "who?"

Vijay said, "He told me his name is Jayant."

"Oh, how was he looking?"

"He was slim, 5.6 feet tall, with fair skin and plane middle-class clerk type person, but his clothes were in a bit of a tattered and slightly soiled condition."

"My God, he must be our Jayant." Manvendra Singh was also there. Thakur Virendra Singh asked him, "What do you think, couldn't he be our Jayant?"

"Yes, he might be."

Vijay asked, "Who is Jayant?"

Thakur Virendra Singh replied, "He is, or I should say, was working in our transport company as an assistant manager. I sent him to Nagpur for a business deal, because I was busy at the wedding. He had one million cash with him. He went there and stayed at the Hotel Continental, but when he was to go to the person to make the deal, he disappeared along with the money. There he befriended a girl, who was also staying in the same hotel, that girl and his father also disappeared. The father-daughter had given false identities there. Now he met you and tried to give you information about Dilip's case. I just can't understand what it is?"

Vijay asked, "In which police station you had lodged the complaint?"

"None."

"What?"

"Yes, I didn't lodge a complaint."

"Why?"

"I don't want to publicize it. That way our rival will know about the dealing. I don't want to disclose it at this stage."

"In that way, how do you recover your money?"

"This dealing is more important to me than recovering the money?"

"OK, as you like. Now what?"

"I can't even think what I should do."

"One thing I can tell you uncle that Jayant didn't steal this amount, otherwise, he didn't try to help you. Something is fishy there."

"You may be right." Thakur Virendra Singh heaved a sigh.

Manvendra Singh asked, "Then it means we still don't know the culprit."

"Yes, but how long he will be unknown? Let's see. Now I have to solve not only Dilip's case but this stealing also. And Uncle there must be a black sheep with you, otherwise, how did all the information passed to the culprits?"

He picked Arhan up on his battery-operated black scooter from there and they left for their home. Arhan asked, "What happened to you exactly?"

"Someone hit me on my head from the back, so I couldn't see him. Jayant must have seen him, but we don't know where he is?"

"He who hit you, how he knew you would be there?"

"Maybe he was behind Jayant, when he got a chance he hit me and fetch Jayant with him, or knew this all from Uncle's end. God knows what happened to Jayant. I think I should get help from Uncle Hameed in that Nagpur case. He may get information about the Hotel, Jayant, that girl, and other involved persons."

"Yes, you are right."

He dropped Arhan at his home and said Arhan to see in the house if Uncle Hameed is there. Arhan came out in a minute and told that Hameed is at home so he went to meet him. He told Hameed all about Thakur Virendra

Singh, Jayant, the transport company, Nagpur, the hotel, the girl, etc. But he had hidden everything about going to Gorai Beach and meeting Jayant there. He knew if he told that he was attacked there and got unconscious that would create problems for him, and he may be restricted strictly to roaming free.

Hameed said, "Hmm... I have a friend in Nagpur, I'll ask him to inquire about it."

Vijay thanks him and left for his home and reached there in minutes.

Hameed called Vijay, "Hello, where are you?"

"Uncle, I'm at home."

"Can you come here?"

"OK, I'm coming."

Vijay reached Hameed's office. Someone was in his room, so he seated out of Hameed's office to wait. After a few minutes, Hameed called him and Vijay entered the room and seated before Hameed. Hameed said, "My Nagpur friend gave me a report that the story of Nagpur that you told me is correct. Jayant also vanished into thin air after that girl and her father. Money is missing as well. Report says that the money was stealed by that girl and his father. Now tell Thakur Virendra Singh to lodge a complaint. Without that, the police couldn't help him."

Vijay said in a troubled tone, "I already told him, but he said the deal is a secret. If he lodged a complaint, it will reveal to his competitors and the deal will slip out of his hands. That will be a bigger jolt than this loss."

Hameed shrugged his shoulders, "OK, it's his money. Let him decide. What can we do?"

7

It was Manvendra Singh's home. A simple home, like a middle-class family has, no interiors were done.

Dharmendra Singh, the general manager of Nashik transport, was there. A glass was before both of them. Dharmendra Singh didn't touch his glass. As a mark of respect, Manvendra Singh also did not touch his glass but kept glancing furtively at his glass again and again.

Dharmendra said, "Look, I can't bear to drink this filthy whisky. I like scotch. You also will afford that after this job. Until that, if you want to drink this, take it and tell me how the job is going on that our company has given you?"

"I'm doing all the needed, be assured," Manvendra Singh replied but still didn't touch his glass.

"But to make Nashik transport no. 1 in the field, you must do something different."

"What?"

"Accident."

"Accident?"

"Yes. After years of thought we reach the conclusion that your company's trucks must meet accidents, in that way people's consignments will not reach timely on the destination, they will be annoyed with your company and our company will be benefited in getting business. And not only this, in that way when Thakur Virendra Singh will try to collect claims from the insurance company, and when it happens regularly, the insurance company will definitely think they are being duped by the transport company and they will investigate it. The accidents must be the way that at the first sight, they look accident but when investigate they shall be looked as designed by someone, and obviously that someone would be Thakur Virendra Singh. It is called two birds with one stone."

"OK. I'll see what can be done in the matter, but I have a question."

"What?"

"Why do you want to frame Thakur Virendra Singh?"

"It's my burning desire to see him behind the bar."

"Why?"

Dharmendra gritted his teeth with anger and hatred, and hissed, "Although it's none of your business, I'll tell you, my father and Virendra Singh's father were cousins. My dad left home in his teenage life. He came to Bombay and started this transport business. That was the Second World War time, and even the government wanted transport so his business developed quadruple speed by day and night. Because he knows English and he made befriended several English people, mostly military officers. Dad used to go to a club; there he made more English civilian officer friends. Because of that, he got so many transport contracts, that he and his staff had to work day and night.

"My dad worked hard. He used to work in his transport office day and night. All night he used to work, even he used to sleep there. But he never missed going to the club in the evening. There he felt fresh and returned to the transport office to drown in the work.

"At that time, he called Virendra Singh to come and help with the work. Obeying him, he came to Bombay. He lived with my dad and work in the transport office. His coming here made a magical effect on business, and it improved to double.

"After that India became independent. Around that time Virendra Singh started his own transport company. Virendra Singh was attached to freedom fighters from the very beginning. So, instantly he was getting government contracts, and he was friendly with businessmen so he was getting business from them and within years he became no. 1 in the field.

"That's why I hate him. He snatched away our business, our position. I can't bear it. I will ruin him. You don't know, even no one knows that the kidnapping of Suraj was actually my plan. I used to feed hate into Dilip's mind against Suraj and Virendra Singh. I used to tell Dilip that when Suraj will mature, Virendra Singh will hand over him all the business and property. He will be merely an employee then.

"I encouraged him to drink with me; I introduced him to the kidnapper and told Dilip that he can do anything for money. And one day, while drunk, he ordered the kidnapper to kidnap Suraj, and he did it as told. While returning from the job, he met an accident and got killed otherwise Thakur Virendra Singh would find him at that time. Unfortunately, one day Dilip saw the will, in which half the property was in his name. Then he himself tried to find Suraj and encouraged his brother to try hard to find Suraj. And one fateful day that snake baby Vijay came into his contact and found Suraj.

"And you know about Jayant. I had sent an offer to buy a transport company from Nagpur to Thakur Virendra Singh from Mr. Agrawal, Nagpur. Thakur Virendra Singh got caught in this trap and sent Jayant there with one million rupees to deal with the offer. Then I sent Ramlal and Kamala to rob those One million Rs. They have done the job beautifully but talking to Jayant somehow Kamala told him her Mumbai address. She made a big mistake, but fortunately, that fixed automatically when instead of going to the police or to Thakur Virendra Singh he followed Kamala and find her in her home and she again made him unconscious and kept him in her house. He escaped from there. Later he was caught in the act of meeting Vijay. Now he knew all about our plans, your roguery, and everything.

We can't afford to let him go out of our captivation. We have to kill him but not now. When the time will come, he will go to the last abode. Till then he must be captivated.

"I want revenge on all of them Virendra Singh, Dilip Singh, Suraj, Jayant, and Vijay. I will not leave anybody. You work for me in the matter and I'll make you a multi-millionaire."

"Yes, I'm ready. Anytime."

"OK. Try such accidents. If you want any help or the manpower, tell me."

"Sure. Now I'll go."

"Good night."

"Good night."

The very next day, a truck of Bombay transport fell into the Godavari River from a bridge. The truck and the consignment were washed away and the driver somehow managed to escape. Manvendra Singh himself went to Thakur Virendra Singh's home to give the news.

"A bad news has come." Manvendra Singh said as he sat before Thakur Virendra Singh. That's why I personally came to inform you."

"What is it?" He said calmly.

"A loaded truck swept away. Fortunately, the driver somehow managed to escape."

"OK. No problem. Claim to the insurance company and paid compensation to the consignees. It's routine, you know it."

"Yes, I know, but I thought I should come and tell you myself."

"There was no need to come, you could tell it on the phone."

"Right, goodbye," and he left.

After a week, Manvendra Singh was sitting before Thakur Virendra Singh and saying, "Bombay transport's another three trucks met accidents in a week." Thakur Virendra Singh looked tense. He further said, "Another bad news is the insurance company refused to pay our claims. They said we are investigating, how so many accidents happened suddenly."

Thakur Virendra Singh was tense. He said, "Earlier there was Dileep's problem, and now this additional problem has arisen. The claims shall be paid or not, but to avoid ruining the business, we have to pay compensation to the consignees from our own pocket. You know if once a party is gone, it never returns. These accidents worried me as well. I never hear it happen earlier, neither in our transport company nor in any other."

"Now, what should we do?" Manvendra asked.

"First of all, we have to take care of our business. We can't afford to lose our parties. Pay all the consignees, whatever they have lost in these accidents. And talk to our lawyer, the agent, who bought the policies for our trucks, and the manager of the insurance company for the claims. Tell them if they will not co-operate with us, then why should we buy their policies? We will not only stop buying their policies but also ask other transporters to boycott them."

"OK, I'll do it, but I don't think the manager of the insurance company will do anything for us, because he said that the instructions have come from the head office, and he is helpless."

"All right, talk to others."

On the other hand, Manvendra Singh was talking to Dharmendra Singh, "Tonight our hugest truck is going to Delhi fully loaded, if it met an accident, The Bombay transport will be ruined because the insurance company wouldn't pass claim and Thakur Virendra Singh doesn't have such a huge amount to pay the compensation from his own pocket."

"OK. Give me the details."

"It's on this paper. Take it." He said giving an envelope to Dharmendra Singh.

"Good. Now I'll take care of the truck."

It was 11.30 at the night, and the closed truck, or should say the container of Bombay transport, was going at a slow pace in silence. There lay the open jungle, with its broad green canopy, bathed in the lovely light of the full moon, sailing aloft in a cloudless sky. The night was very warm, and the headlight of the container was helpless to show ahead on the road. The black tar road and the surrounding area were not better lighted, so the driver of the container was looking ahead with fully opened eyes. A truck was passing by its side. Ramlal was in the passing truck with his gang. As the truck was going to pass, both trucks were running side by side. Ramlal and his gang were at the top of the cabin of this truck. While passing, they hold the container body with their hands and climbed up.

Vijay was also in the driver's cabin of the container with Captain Hameed. Their presence has a reason. Yesterday, he came to meet Thakur Virendra Singh to discuss the case. There, Thakur Virendra Singh told him about accidents and expressed his suspicion, "I haven't listened in my life, so many accidents in such a short period." He further said, "I fear, tomorrow there is a huge consignment going to Delhi. It's the biggest truck in our transport company. If someone is behind all these things, he certainly will try to do something to the truck to meet an accident. What should I do?"

Vijay consoled, "Don't worry uncle, I'll do something." That's why he was there with Hameed because he told all this to him and asked for his help.

Hameed heard some sound and became alert and ordered the driver to keep running. He instantly took out his revolver from his pocket and in the running truck opened the truck door and tried to climb up. He saw two people and ordered, "Hands up." And instead of two, five pairs of hands went up. Hameed had seen only two people, whereas there were five people on the roof of the truck actually.

After Hameed, Vijay too climbed up as well. He photographed all five people with his mobile in night mode. Then even video-graphed them for solid proof."

Now again the truck that was passed their container slowed and came side by side. Unfortunately, the container jolted, and the revolver fell from Hameed's hand. Seizing the opportunity, the gang of Ramlal jumped into their truck and before Hameed can do anything, the truck stopped and took a U-turn, and ran away in the back direction fast. Hameed took his revolver and saw toward Vijay. Vijay was saying to stop the truck to the driver. The driver stopped the truck. It took two minutes. Hameed asked, "What happened?"

Vijay replied, "My mobile fell down from the truck. I have photographed and video-graphed them. We can find and prosecute them based on that."

"Oh. But would their faces be recognized, because there was dark?"

"Yes, of course, I had used the night mode."

Both got down and headed in the coming direction. A powerful torch was in Hameed's hands. They were looking for the mobile in the torch's light. Soon they found the mobile, but it was useless, the mobile was broken. Vijay picked up the mobile and was looking at it in dismay.

Hameed said, "No problem. We can show it to a good mobile repairer. He may fix it. Let's go, to stand here is useless, let's move."

They returned to the truck, stopped the truck at the nearest town, and alighted there. Hameed said, "Now there is no risk of attack for the second time on the truck. We'll return to Mumbai from here."

They were going towards the settlement area. Hameed was whistling his favorite song from the Hollywood film 'Come September.' A patrolling constable stopped them and asked who they were and where they were going at that time of the night. Hameed told him they were headed to the police station.

The constable said, "I'll take you there."

The town was a tiny one or a big village. Everything was under the darkness cover except street lights and a few houses have low light in their courtyard. They reached the police station, which was also an old construction, where Hameed introduced himself and asked about what can be the means to go back to Mumbai. He was told that they can get a bus, but at this time it was not possible, they have to wait until morning. He asked, "OK, is there any hotel or something to relax for the rest of the night?"

The head constable replied in affirmative. Hameed said, "Please, show us a good one."

He said, "Sir, there is only one, say it good or bad."

Hameed said, "OK. What cannot be cured just be endured."

A constable led them to the hotel; it was a simple two-story building. Here they registered and went to sleep; it was another matter that they could not sleep because there were mosquitoes in the room. They tried to fully cover themselves with sheets but that was useless as well. When they cover their faces they felt better but for a few minutes only, because after that they felt suffocation and they had to uncover their faces and again they had to bear mosquito bites and their rhythmless music.

The next day they got up. It was a lovely morning, sunny and calm; but because of less sleep, Hameed looked listless and fatigued, placed on a comfortable easy chair near the window, from whence he could see one of the prettiest flowers, grass, and trees of the garden, gay with flowers of every colour and fragrance. Vijay remained standing, one hand resting lightly on a table.

Hameed saw the grass full of dew as pearls on the grass and the grass looked white instead of green, the drooping boughs of trees, and straight before their line of vision a little piece of the blessed sky, opal tinted and faintly blushing with the consciousness of the approaching sunrise. They drank in the sweet, fresh air. A long trailing branch of the wild grapevine hung near the window; its leaves were covered thickly with dew. Vijay squeezed one hand through the grating and gathered a few of these green morsels of coolness. He devoured them. It seemed to him more delicious than anything he had ever tasted. It relieved his parched throat and tongue. The glimpse of the trees and sky soothed and calmed them. There was a gentle twittering of awaking birds. The nightingale had ceased singing.

After the shops were opened, Hameed went to a general store to buy toothpaste and two toothbrushes. The hotel didn't provide them with that. Even Vijay went to the counter in the night for some mosquito repellent and was told that they don't have any.

Then he asked, "So, how can we sleep?"

They replied, "As we are sleeping."

They were sleeping with covers on their faces. Vijay returned empty-handed from there because he already had tried the trick to cover the face and found it useless. The hotel was with very basic amenities only, not even room service and a room telephone. Anyway, the hotel provided them with towels and soap, so after getting ready, they went to the bus stop to go to Mumbai. They had to wear the same clothes as they had not brought other clothes with them and Hameed thought clothes bought here would be a nightmare experience.

They had breakfast and tea at the bus stop before boarding the bus. For breakfast, they ordered misal-pav, a regional meal like a curry but with an excessive amount of chilly and two little loaves of bread. It had so much chilly that Vijay's eyes welled up with tears while eating. After that Hameed buy some peda (A sweet), then they took tea which tasted like a sweet dish because it was overly sugary.

When a bus arrived, they boarded it and reached home in the evening.

After reaching home, Vijay reported to Thakur Virendra Singh. Manvendra Singh was also with Thakur Virendra Singh and listening to their conversation on the phone. Vijay said, "Now I have photos of the gangsters who attacked the truck."

"What, you have photos of those gangsters?"

"Yes, but I can't show you at the moment, because while taking photos my mobile dropped and broke. Tomorrow I'll go to a mobile repairer and see what can be done."

"Oh. OK, see you. Good night."

"Good night uncle."

"What happened, Thakur sahib?" Manvendra asked.

“Oh, nothing, Vijay was telling that he photographed the gangsters, who attacked the truck, but his mobile broke, he will take it to a mobile repairer and will repair it, and then we can know the attackers.”

“Is he going now to the mobile repairer?”

“No, he said, he will go tomorrow.”

“OK. Let me go to the office.”

“All right, go away.”

Manvendra Singh came out of the house and started his car. Going around a km. he stopped the car and called Dharmendra Singh, “Hello, Vijay has photographs of Ramlal and his team members who attacked the truck, but fortunately, the mobile in which were photos, is broken, he will go to repair it tomorrow. Do something.”

“OK. I’ll do, whatever is needed.”

8

The next day, Vijay was going to repair the mobile with Balwant, on his battery-operated black scooter. A white colour Tata Indica car was behind them. At a deserted place, the car accelerated, and before Vijay could react, it collided with his scooter. Vijay and Balwant fell on one side and the scooter on the other side and a mobile fell on his side from the shirt’s front pocket of Vijay. From the car two people ran to Vijay, their eyes fell on the mobile, they grab it and flew to their car and the car fled away.

Vijay was lying on the ground; he stood up from the ground. He has seen that two people grabbing the mobile. Strangely, instead of being upset, he smiled. He understood they were behind the mobile, but the mobile that has photos was in the scooter’s boot. The mobile which they grabbed was another mobile he fetched with him to call anybody if needed.

Balwant fell with him and both of them only got some bruises here and there; there weren't any serious injuries. Actually, Balwant told him last night that a friend of his father, who belongs to his village in Panjab, has a mobile shop and he also repairs mobiles. Balwant saw his smile and asked, "What happened? Why are you smiling?"

Vijay said, "The mobile that we were to going repair is safe in the scooter's boot."

"What? And the mobile they fetched with them?"

"That was another phone I brought for normal use if needed."

"Oh."

"So, let's move to uncle's shop."

"Yes."

They picked up the fallen scooter and headed to the shop. Seeing Balwant, the owner of the shop, Sardar Satram Singh, shouted with joy, "Hey Balwant, how are you? What are you doing here? And who is with you?"

"Uncle I'm fine. He is my friend Vijay, we came to you for a mobile, which fell and broke."

"OK. Show me."

Vijay opened the boot, took out the mobile, and placed it in front of Satram Singh.

He checked and said, "It will be very costly to repair, better get a new one."

Vijay said, "There are very important photos in it. That's why I want to repair it."

"Don't you have a memory card in it?"

"No, it has ample space so I didn't buy one."

"Oh, if you had the card and the photos you taken were stored in that then you didn't have to repair it."

"I know Uncle but I didn't need so... Anyway there is no use of cry over spilt milk now," Vijay sighed.

"OK, in an hour my technician shall come and he will repair it. But it will take time; I'll have to arrange its parts."

Vijay said "OK' and he returned with Balwant. Midway they decided to go to Thakur Virendra Singh, so Vijay turned the scooter that way.

They were sitting before Thakur Virendra Singh, and Manvendra Singh was also presented. Vijay told him about the mobile and an attempt to snatch it and how by mistake the wrong mobile was snatched. Thakur Virendra Singh said, "Oh, my, my."

Vijay added, "Within days, the phone will be amended, and we may know who the culprits are."

Manvendra Singh said, "Let me go to the office." And he left.

Vijay asked, "He spends much time here, no?"

"Yes, he doesn't have to be in the office, so used to come here or sometimes I call him because nowadays I rarely go to the office. Actually, he belongs to our native place. His father was my father's good friend. So he is just like a family member."

"You are right; believe that is why you agreed to marry his daughter to Dilip uncle?"

"In a way yes," Thakur Virendra Singh replied.

Vijay bluffed, "Yesterday when I called about the mobile that time also I listened to his voice."

"Yes he was here and I told him about the mobile and photos."

Today, in the evening, Vijay called Thakur Virendra Singh, "Hello, uncle, I'm coming to your home to watch the photos and video of those criminals who try to destroy the truck. We can attach the mobile to a laptop or TV because we can't identify those on the tiny mobile screen. Do you have or should I bring with me my laptop?"

"No problem, I have a laptop, but why do you want to watch here?"

"Simple, uncle, you may recognize them."

"Oh, OK. In that case, I call Manvendra as well. He would be a help in recognizing."

"OK, all right. I'll be there at 8.00 PM." He cut the call.

Before 5 minutes to 8.00 PM, Vijay reached there and started attaching the mobile to the laptop. Within minutes, the laptop was on and the mobile was attached. He said to Thakur Virendra Singh, "It's ready, uncle. Should I start or wait for uncle Manvendra?"

"We can wait. He will come. Meanwhile, we can take a cup of tea. What you say."

"As you like, Uncle."

He ordered tea and biscuits, and they were seated and chatting. A maid brought tea and biscuits. They enjoyed tea and biscuits, and then Thakur Virendra Singh said, "I think we may start now. If Manvendra came we may start again or he may watch it later."

"OK," Vijay said and as he was ready to start, the lights went off and a minute later a voice tooted, "Hands up both of you."

It was a muscular person, wearing a mask and holding a gun in hand. He forwarded and took the mobile and laptop and vanished into thin air. Thakur Virendra Singh was looking at Vijay, who has a smile on his face. The smile looks weird to him, but he didn't say anything. Vijay said. "OK. Uncle, I'll go." and he left.

Manvendra Singh was at Dharmendra Singh's home. They were watching the photos on the laptop, brought by Manvendra Singh. Dharmendra Singh, watching this said, "Well done Manvendra, Ramlal is clearly identified, and others as well. If these photos were watched by them we would be in jail. Destroy this mobile immediately"

"Yes," he said and opened the mobile, lit the cigarette lighter, and put the mobile on its flame. After five minutes he threw the mobile in a corner, "Now all its data is finished."

"I'm happy. Your five million or ready, take away whenever you want."

"OK. Give it to me, and I'll go to my home."

Dharmendra Singh gave him a suitcase, and he left.

After five minutes, a call came from Dharmendra Singh. "Hello, I forgot. Now, what is the program?"

"Oh, yes, tomorrow, a truck of Bombay transport is coming from Delhi and a truck is going to Delhi via Western Expressway. If all is well, they will cross each other about 20 Km from Manor around Mendhwan. It's a forest area. If anyhow, the trucks ram each other, it would be fatal for Bombay transport. No one would believe it is an accident. Everyone would think if they both were going on their side, then how come they rammed each other? And both are from the same transport company, so police and the insurance company would certainly think that the accident is manipulated."

"Hmm... You are right I'll do whatever I can."

The next day, Vijay was before Colonel Vinod, his father, at the home. "Well?" Vinod asked.

Vijay told him everything about his adventure. Vinod asked, "You did it without asking me, then why do you telling me all this now?"

"I came to know that today two trucks of Bombay transport will meet an accident."

Vinod sat upright. "How do you know this?"

"I have fitted a gadget in Manvendra Singh's car. Yester night he was telling on the mobile to create the accident."

"Do you know where they had planned to create this accident?"

"Yes. Ahead of the western Expressway. Trucks will cross each other about 20 km from Manor around Mendhwan. It's a forest area."

"So, what do you want?"

"If we could prevent this accident from happening?"

"Of course, we can. But, in that case, we couldn't punish them, because the crime will not have been committed, so the court will scott them free because creating an accident shall be their intention and no court will punish a person on the intention. It will punish only for the crime committed, not for the intentions. The other thing is how can we prove that they have the intention of creating an accident?"

"It doesn't matter. I have some evidence against them."

"What?"

"The photos of the criminals who tried to create an accident the other day."

"But you said that mobile was snatched away from you?"

"Yes, but I was aware that some sort of event can be committed, so I have copied all the data to a memory card."

"That's great. Give me that card. And let me first try to prevent the accident."

"Thanks, dad."

Vinod started the preparations immediately for the evening. From Mendhwan to 50 km south he held the command in his hands and up to 50 km north he had given the command to Hameed. He gave the instructions to both teams. Vinod and Hameed both were in police cars with force.

As the truck of Bombay transport crossed Vinod's vehicle, he ordered to follow it from a long distance. Two cops were posted every five Km. with motorcycles. All were connected with walkie-talkies. Vinod was listening to them carefully. The cops, posted 20 km before Mendhwan, said excitedly, "Sir, a car has come to a stop in front of the truck and the truck has also stopped due to the car. And now people in the car alighted and attacking to the truck."

Vinod ordered, the driver to go fast, at the first sentence of the cops. He said, "Attack on them but don't fire on them directly. We are to arrest them alive."

Before his order, his car had also come to the scene. He and his colleagues also fired in the air. The attackers panicked and they surrendered. Police arrested them on the charge of attacking the truck for trying to loot and truck theft.

9

Vijay's phone's screen flashed, and for an unknown reason, his ringtone and vibration weren't functioning. He replied, "Hello."

"Hello, this is Manvendra Singh. Would you please come here?" was said from the other end. I have something to show you."

"OK, I'll be there."

He turned off his phone and informed Balwant, with whom he was sharing a coffee in a café that he was going to meet Manvendra Singh at his house. He invited me, but it seems to me a trap. You come along with me near his house, I'll enter the home, if I will not emerge within half an hour; inform papa or Hameed uncle or your papa. OK?"

"It's OK, but why are you taking the risk? Why don't you call the police?"

"We don't have any evidence against him, so the police can't do anything. If he does anything unlawful, then we will have the evidence and we will catch him."

"OK. If you say so. Go ahead."

Miss Marple was in the market with her mother, Agatha. They came for some shopping. She saw Ramlal going into a shop. She thought she had seen him somewhere, but where, she couldn't recall. After four-five minutes she got a brain wave that she had not seen him but his photos, in the possession of Vijay, who told her they were criminals and were trying to make an accident of trucks.

She said to her mother, "Mom, you go ahead, I'll come."

She returned to that shop and was standing before a vegetable vendor's shop that was opposite that shop. She was afraid that the criminal may have gone. But her waiting paid off, and the fellow appeared. He went to one side and got an auto rickshaw.

Miss Marple quickly went to where her mother parked her scooter. The keys were with Marple. She started the scooter and headed in the direction where the auto went. The auto was going slow because the road was crowded with people and small vendors. Within seconds, she saw the auto, and she started following the auto.

The auto reached a small house on the outskirts of the suburb. That fellow entered the house, but the auto was still there. After four-five minutes, he came back and left in the auto. In between, Marple inquired about the house and the fellow, from a girl of her age, in a cosmetic shop. The fellow was Ramlal, a local goon, who lived with his daughter Kamala, who also helps in her father's jobs.

Now the daylight was gone, and it was the golden darkness of the dusk. Some shopkeepers had switched on their shop lights. She quietly went backside of the house. It was too filthy, but she reached the rear of the house. She saw the back door was not shut properly. She peeped inside, but there wasn't anyone, so she entered and heard some voices from a room. The door of the room was closed.

They were the young voices of a male and a female. She peeped from the keyhole of the door. She saw a young boy around 26-28 in torn clothes, seated in a chair. She peeped on and saw that he was not a free man; He was a captive person, and his hands were tied to the arms of the chair.

But the girl couldn't be seen from the keyhole. She began to think, now what to do? She was a daredevil, but still; Marple was a little scared because that girl was unseen, and an unseen thing always is more dangerous. Another thing, she was thinking about that fellow Ramlal, who went somewhere; she doesn't know when he will come. He may come any moment.

But she continued snooping. She saw a half-opened window; it was the window of the same room the voices were coming from. She tiptoed towards the window and with too much care she peeped through the window. The girl that was talking to the boy was walking while talking. She was around 24-26, with a fair complexion, and wore a pant and a t-shirt. She tried to look like a lady, but she could not hide the cheapness in her gestures. Marple now can clearly hear what was saying on. She heard the girl say, "OK, I'm going to make a cup of tea for you." And she left the room.

Marple assumed if she went to make tea that means it will take 5-7 minutes for her to come back. She slowly entered the room and pointed a finger at the lips to keep the boy quiet and began to untie his hands that were tied with a cord.

Suddenly there was a sound of someone coming and Marple hid behind the same chair because there was no other place to hide. It was the same girl who came and asked from the door itself, "Should I bring you some biscuits as well?"

He said, "Yes, please, and thanks."

And she returned to the kitchen. She didn't see his hands; otherwise, she would have understood that someone had opened the card. That boy was freed in a minute. They both came out of the room and before the girl can return, they were out of the house.

Coming out, he told that his name is Jayant and Marple understood everything, she took him to the nearest police station on the scooter. The police inspector asked for Jayant's statement but Marple told that Colonel Vinod is investigating this case and the police should immediately raid the house and arrest all the people present there, otherwise they will flee from the house.

When the police inspector knew that the commissioner of police, Colonel Vinod was involved in the case. He act quickly and surrounded the house. The police inspector announced on the mic, "This house is surrounded on all sides. Come out with your hands up or else we will not be responsible for the consequences."

The Inspector repeated the announcement and when he was ready to force his way into the house, Kamala, Ramlal, and their five goons came out with their hands up. The police handcuffed them and took them to the police station.

Vijay and Balwant reached the house of Manvendra Singh on Vijay's battery-operated black scooter. Balwant alighted a little earlier. Vijay alone entered the house. Manvendra Singh was sitting alone waiting for him with a glass of drink. He said, "Welcome, welcome, Vijay. I was waiting for you."

"Is there anything I can do for you?"

"No, nothing. I'll tell you and show you some interesting things. First of all, I'm one of the culprits of the game that you already know."

Vijay nodded.

Manvendra Singh added, ignoring him, "I least bother about your knowledge because I'm leaving this country in half an hour." He gave a wicked grin.

"You may be curious why I'm telling you all this. First, you have harmed me a lot, so I must punish you for it. No?" Suddenly a pistol flashed in his hand.

Vijay raised his hands up. Manvendra Singh again smiled, "Now, I tell you the great mystery of the game," he called, "Baby."

And within seconds, Chandrika came there slowly. Her face was white and she seems very frightened. She said slowly, "Papa, I still suggest you, don't do this."

Vijay stared in disbelief. Everyone believes she is dead and he sees her in flesh and bone.

"You still would be amazed why I'm telling you all my secrets, no?" Manvendra Singh said. "I'm telling you because you are going to die and we are leaving this country. A vessel is waiting in international waters. We are going there in a boat."

He ordered Vijay to go to another room. He closed Vijay into that room and said, "Now a cobra will enter the room. It depends on you, how you can save yourself. Goodbye."

Balwant saw Manvendra Singh with a lady, leaving the house, but there was no sign of Vijay. He thought about entering the house to find Vijay, but he didn't know how many people were there and what happened to Vijay. Quickly he decided to call Colonel Vinod, as Vijay had told him to do. He called Vinod and told him that Vijay may be in danger. Vinod told him don't enter the house, and that he was coming as soon as possible.

Vinod rushed there. Balwant was waiting for him. Vinod said to him to wait there and entered the house with a pistol in his hand and ready for any incident.

Vijay was in a dimly lit room. A minute later, a cobra was entering from the skylight. Vijay didn't move at all. He has seen many snakes in Vinod's bungalow, so he was not scared. The room was totally empty, so he couldn't think of how to counter the cobra. And he heard Vinod's voice from the door. He shouted, "Papa, I'm here, and beware, a cobra is also here."

Vinod broke down the door and took stock standing at the door. He entered the room and within a minute, the cobra was clenched in his hands. He put it in a box, found in another room. Then he asked Vijay about the case and Vijay told him everything in short and that Manvendra Singh was about to leave India with his daughter.

Vinod was startled to hear 'Manvendra's daughter.' He asked to confirm, "Manvendra's daughter?"

"Yes father, she didn't agree with his plans but he took her by force."

"Do you mean Chandrika?"

"Yes, exactly the same."

"OK, Go home I'll see what can I do. But no, come with me. You know him, so you shall be a help in identifying him."

They came out, and Vinod asked, "Now, where."

Vijay replied, "He was saying, he would leave India in half an hour. I think he must have gone to Mahim Creek. There he would have arranged a boat and he could board any large launch or ship that is anchored in international waters."

"Good, your conclusion is right, like a detective."

Vinod alerted the coastguards, and when they reach there, a motorboat was waiting for them. They came out to the open sea. Three vessels were anchored there. Other than these vessels, there were some motor boats for coastguards. Manvendra could have planned his escape from one of these three ships.

Vijay was thinking, is Manvendra reached already any of these ships? In that case, they couldn't do anything to find him, because these ships were in international waters.

Suddenly, they saw a black dinghy approaching a vessel. The black dinghy appeared for a few seconds and then disappeared into the black sea. It was enough for Vinod. His boat made its way there while turning on its searchlight. That dinghy became clearly visible.

Apart from Vinod's motorboat, others also surrounded the dinghy from all sides. Manvendra Singh and his daughter Chandrika were arrested from the dinghy.

The next day's newspapers were full of Manvendra Singh's arrest. Colonel Vinod, Captain Hameed, and The Fab Four team members all gathered at Thakur Virendra Singh's house along with Thakur Virendra Singh, Suraj alias Asst. professor Jay Sharma, Professor Rajan Sharma, Manisha, and Jayant.

Vijay told them, "I got suspicious about Manvendra Singh when I went to meet Jayant and there I was attacked and Jayant was kidnapped. Then I fit a gadget in his car and I knew he wanted to ruin Bombay transport. At first, I think he is doing this because his daughter was murdered, but later I came to know that he was doing all this for money."

Vinod told them, "Dharmendra Singh of Nashik transport is arrested. He is the mastermind of it all. He was even the brain behind the kidnapping of Suraj. Jayant escaped from Ramlal's house. He told the police everything. One million are recovered from there. You may claim it," He said, turning to Thakur Virendra Singh.

Further, he said, "Dilip Singh will be released in a day with the court's permission. And though Chandrika was innocent, it'll take time to release her because she was involved in the conspiracy of her fake murder. She was deceived by his father, but the law does not believe in these things, so it will take some time for her to be released from jail."

Thakur Virendra Singh said, "All's well that ends well. I think Dilip shall also pardon her. But I am still sad that Dharmendra is arrested, after all, he is my brother. Is there no possibility he could be released, Colonel? Maybe he too will be a good chap like Dilip"

"I will say one thing," Hameed said, "I want to ask Jayant, now what he thinks about Kamala?"

Jayant replied with seriousness, "I hope now she will be a good girl and she will give up all wrongdoing and I will accept her and will marry her after her release from jail."

Suraj said, "Now, you all were returned from my marriage without the party, so let's start the party."

The End

Printed by Libri Plureos GmbH in Hamburg, Germany

9 798889 591061